For Elsie and Emile —M. R.

For Emily —A. R.

Text copyright © 2009 by Michael Rosen
Illustrations copyright © 2009 by Adrian Reynolds

First published in Great Britain in 2009 by Bloomsbury Publishing Plc.
Published in the United States in 2009 by Bloomsbury U.S.A. Children's Books
175 Fifth Avenue, New York, New York 10010

Library of Congress Cataloging-in-Publication Data
Rosen, Michael.
Bear flies high / by Michael Rosen. — 1st U.S. ed.
p.   cm.
Summary: Bear usually spends his days on the beach, singing and watching birds,
but when he leaves to visit a carnival, his dream of flying may just come true.
ISBN-13: 978-1-59990-386-6 • ISBN-10: 1-59990-386-5 (hardcover)
ISBN-13: 978-1-59990-387-3 • ISBN-10: 1-59990-387-3 (reinforced)
[1. Bears—Fiction. 2. Flight—Fiction. 3. Amusement rides—Fiction. 4. Carnivals—Fiction.] I. Title.
PZ7.R71867Bdm 2009   [E]—dc22   2008055015

Typeset in Temble ITC
Art created with watercolor

First U.S. Edition 2009
Printed in China by Printplus Limited
2 4 6 8 10 9 7 5 3 1 (hardcover)
2 4 6 8 10 9 7 5 3 1 (reinforced)

All papers used by Bloomsbury U.S.A. are natural, recyclable products
made from wood grown in well-managed forests. The manufacturing processes
conform to the environmental regulations of the country of origin.

Bear Flies High

Michael Rosen

illustrated by Adrian Reynolds

BLOOMSBURY

NEW YORK BERLIN LONDON

I'm a bear on a beach.
On a beach?
On a beach.

And I sing by the sea all day.
Doo bee doo
Doo bee doo
Doo bee doodily doo.

I watch the birds in the sky.
In the sky?
In the sky.

And they fly above me up high.
Swoopy swoop
Swoopy swoop
Swoopy swoopity swoop.

I wish I could fly up high.
Up high?
Up high!

I wish I could fly up high one day.
Swoopy swoop
Swoopy swoop
Swoopy swoopity swoop.

"If you want to fly, Mr. Bear, follow us."
"Follow you?"
"Follow us.
    Follow us to a place far away."

Follow, follow

Follow, follow

Follow follity follow.

We're waiting at the gate.
At the gate?
At the gate.

We're waiting at the gate to get in.
Don't push!
Don't push!
Don't pushy push!

Cups and saucers whirling round.
Whirling round?
Whirling round.

Cups and saucers whirling round all day.
Whirly whirl
Whirly whirl
Whirly whirlity whirl.

Haunted house whooping loud.
Whooping loud?
Whooping loud.

Haunted house whooping loud all day.
Hoo woo
Hoo woo
Hoo woopity woo!

Big flipper flying high.
Flying high?
Flying high.

Big flipper flying high in the sky.
Whooshy whoosh
Whooshy whoosh
Whooshy whooshy whoosh.

"You can fly up there, Mr. Bear."
"Up there?"
"Up there.
    You can fly up there, if you dare."

Scary scare

Scary scare

Scary scarety scare.

I'm a bear who can fly!
You can fly?
I can fly.

I can fly in the sky like a bird up high.
Swoopy swoop
Swoopy swoop
Swoopy swoopity swoop.

Then it's back down the road.
Down the road?
Down the road.

Back down the road to get home.
Follow follow
Follow follow
Follow follity follow.

We watch the birds in the sky.
In the sky?
In the sky.
We watch the birds in the sky up high.

And we sing by the sea all day.
Doo bee doo
Doo bee doo   Swoopy swoopity swooooooooo